Michael Recycle

www.WorthwhileChildrensBooks.com

ISBN: 978-1-60010-224-0

11 10 09 08   3 4 5 6

Text copyright © 2008 Ellie Bethel.

Illustrations copyright © 2008 Alexandra Colombo.

Published by arrangement with Meadowside Children's Books, 185 Fleet Street, London EC4A 2HS.

Jonas Publishing, Publisher: Howard Jonas • IDW, Chairman: Morris Berger • IDW, President: Ted Adams
Worthwhile Books, Vice-President and Creative Director: Rob Kurtz • Worthwhile Books, Senior Editor: Megan Bryant

IDW & JONAS PUBLISHING

PRESENT:

WORTHWHILE BOOKS

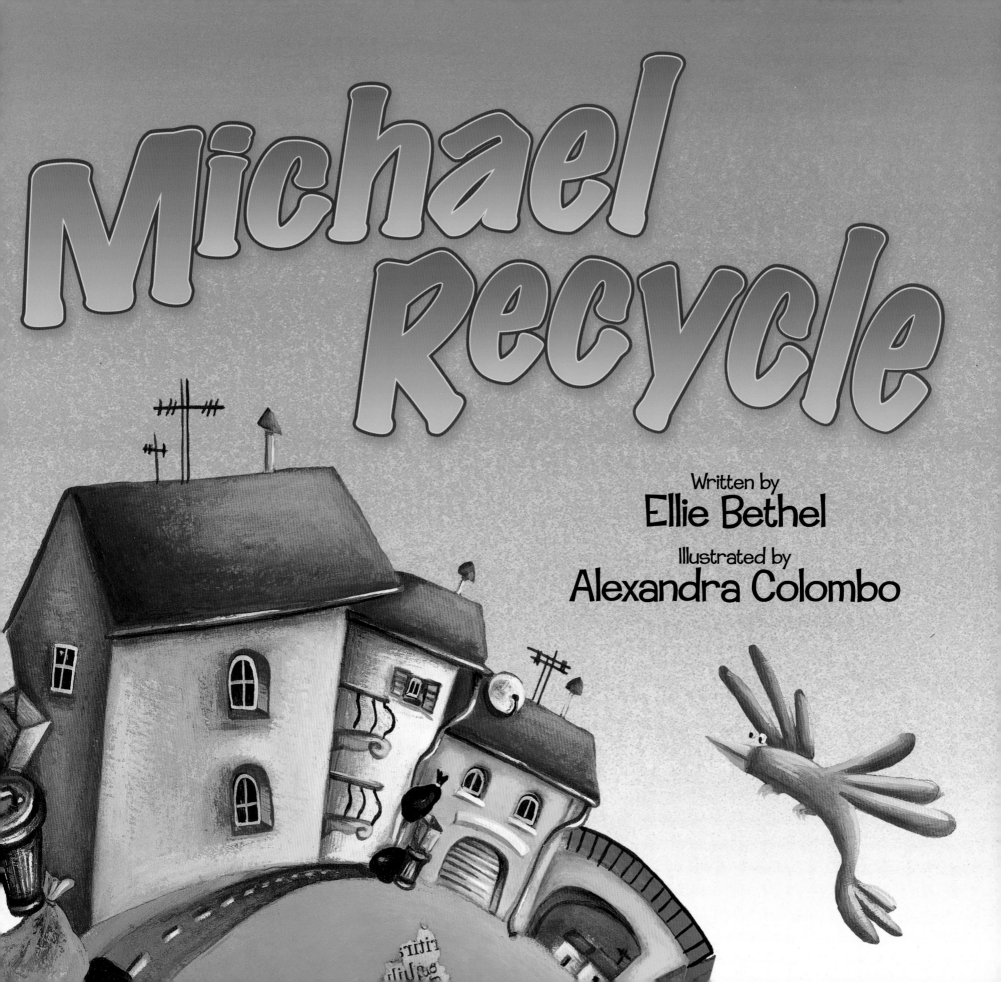

Michael Recycle

Written by
Ellie Bethel

Illustrated by
Alexandra Colombo

For my very own little superheroes,
Daniel, JJ & Ben—E.B.

For Mummy, Daddy (gnome), Pepi & Kay:
my superheroes!—A.C.

There once was a town
Called Abberdoo-Rimey,
Where garbage was left
To grow rotten and slimy.

It never smelled fresh.
The air was all hazy.
But the people did nothing.
**They got
rather lazy.**

And then something happened
That none could explain.
It wasn't a bird
And it wasn't a plane.

A green-caped crusader
Soared through the air,
With a colander hat
On top of his hair.

He bounced off the earth
With a *thump* and a *bump*,
And then landed headfirst
In the town garbage dump.

He brushed off his suit
As he jumped to his feet,
And grinned at the townsfolk
Who he'd come to meet.

"I'm Michael Recycle

And I have a plan.
But I need your help-
Everyone to a man.

The sky and the river
Are smelly and brown.
Soon fifty-foot bugs
Will take over your town!"

"**You've got
to recycle!**
You've got to act soon!
Before all your trash
Reaches up to the moon!"

Then crushing a can,
He gave them a wink...

And vanished from sight
Before they could blink!

Miss Moonkotch exclaimed
To her friend Mr. Crew,
"Did you happen to hear
What that boy said to do?"

"Clean up and recycle—
How hard can it be?
A green and clean town
Would be lovely to see!"

They **recycled** their paper,
Their plastic and cans,
And even old junk
Like used pots and pans!

They also began
The **"Be Greener Campaign."**
They grew their own kumquats
And saved up the rain.

So proud was the town
Of their green transformation
They threw a great party—
A Grand Celebration!

They covered the town
In green toilet paper,
Then rolled it back up
To use again later.

You may think that's yucky,
But these folks don't agree.
In Abberdoo-Rimey,
Recycling is key!

When Michael came back
To visit the town,
He didn't despair,
Get angry, or frown.

For everything looked
So clean and brand-new,
The sky and the river
Were again a bright blue

"Look at our town!
It gleams and it glitters!
Now nothing's wasted
And nobody litters!"

"To Michael Recycle,
The Green-Caped Crusader!
Our super-green hero.
**The planet's
new savior!"**

But Michael Recycle
Was nowhere around.
He'd already moved on
To help the next town.

So if you should see
A green silhouette
Streaking the skies
Please don't get upset!

The noises you hear—
That *clunk* and that *thunk*—

Michael Recycle's Go green Tips

Recycle, Recycle, Recycle!

Find out what can be recycled in your town—most towns offer curbside pickup for newspapers, cans, glass, and certain kinds of plastic. You might also be able to recycle Styrofoam, foil, cardboard, catalogs and magazines, and even appliances or electronic equipment. Who knows, maybe they'll even take your little brother or sister!

Turn It Off!

Turn off electronic equipment (like the TV, computer, and stereo) when you're not using it.

Recharge It, Please!

Ask your parents to buy rechargeable batteries and energy-efficient lightbulbs.

Don't Be a Drip!

Check all the faucets in your house. If any are dripping, ask your parents to fix them. If they don't do it, tell them you're just concerned about the water bill—they'll be very impressed.

Quick and Clean!

Take shorter showers— unless you're really, really smelly.

No Running, When Brushing!

Turn off the running faucet while you're brushing your teeth.

Take a Stroll!

Whenever you can, walk or ride your bike. Maybe you can get your parents to ride along, too—right beside you.

No Paper Trail!

Reduce the amount of paper you use at home.
Use dishtowels or rags instead of paper towels,
and cloth napkins instead of paper napkins.
Write messages for your family on a wipe-off
board instead of on a notepad.
Use both sides of a piece
of paper before throwing
it out. Tell your parents
that if they don't
conserve paper, you'll run
out and then you won't be
able to do your homework.

Trees, Please!

Trees are true friends of the earth. They keep us cool and make
oxygen for us to breathe. Plant a tree in your yard—or organize
a tree-planting party for your neighborhood or school. At the
very least, say thank you when you pass that big elm or
maple—don't worry, they won't "bark."

Can It!

Don't litter! Make sure your trash ends up where it belongs—in a trash can, or in the back of your closet.

Pile It Up!

Don't throw away grass clippings and fallen leaves—start a compost pile in your backyard! A little sun, a little rain, a few bugs-okay, millions of bugs (which is the cool part!)—and in a few months you'll have healthy soil for your garden. And all those trimmings and clippings won't be taking up space in a landfill. You can add eggshells, coffee grounds, and fruit and vegetable peels to your compost pile, too—but no annoying cousins.

The End